THE WORRY MACHINE

A
FABLES FROM THE LETTER PEOPLE
BOOK

WRITTEN BY:
ELAYNE REISS-WEIMANN
RITA FRIEDMAN

ILLUSTRATED BY:
ELIZABETH CALLEN

NEW DIMENSIONS IN EDUCATION, INC.
50 EXECUTIVE BLVD.
ELMSFORD, NY 10523

Printed in U.S.A.

ISBN 0-89796-022-X

1 2 3 4 5 6 7 8 9 0   SPC   SPC   89098   13523

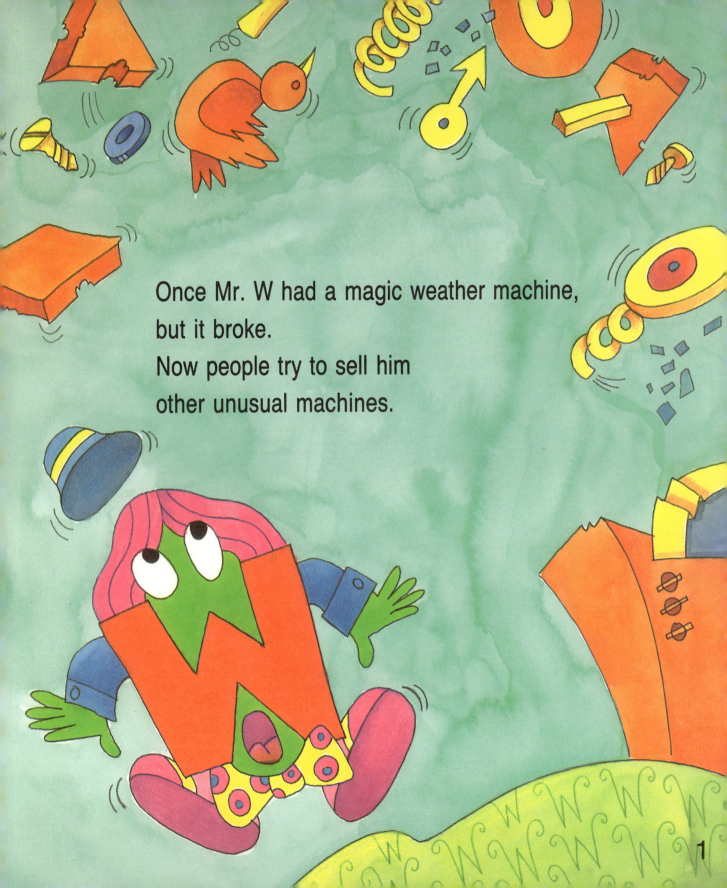

Once Mr. W had a magic weather machine,
but it broke.
Now people try to sell him
other unusual machines.

1

Salespeople come to Mr. W's house every day.
"I have a wonderful waffle machine for you,"
says one salesperson.
"It makes one hundred waffles in one minute."
"I have a wonderful window washing machine,"
says another salesperson.
"It will wash windows without water."
"I don't want any more unusual machines," says Mr. W.
"Unusual machines can be a worry."

3

"Did I hear you say worry?" asks a third salesperson.

"I have just the machine for you.

It is a worry machine," she says.

"You whisper your worry to the machine,

and the machine will tell you what to do."

"A machine can't think," says Mr. W.

"I'll send it to you," says the salesperson.

"If it doesn't work, return it to me."

5

The next day, the worry machine arrives.

The directions say:

"Whisper your worry to the worry machine.

Turn the dial.

Wink one wink.

A white card will drop from the slot.

It will tell you what to do about your worry."

"I can't believe a machine can really help you with worries," says Mr. W.

"But I'll try it."

Mr. W whispers his worry to the machine:

"My friends and I plan to take a walk on Wednesday.

I am worried it may rain."

Mr. W turns the dial.

The worry machine wiggles and whirls.

Mr. W winks one wink.

A white card drops from the slot.

Mr. W picks up the white card and reads it.
The card says, "Don't Worry."
"The worry machine is right," says Mr. W.
"Worrying doesn't solve a problem.
You have to think of what to do.
If it rains this Wednesday, my friends and I will walk next Wednesday.
I won't worry."

The children come to Mr. W's house.

"May we use your worry machine?" they ask.

"You may," says Mr. W, "but one at a time."

First, William and Mr. W go into the den

to use the worry machine.

"Mr. W, I broke my neighbor's window with my ball.

I am worried about what will happen

when she comes home from work," says William.

"Let's talk and think together," says Mr. W.

"We'll solve your problem."

"I didn't mean to break the window," says William.
"Then tell your neighbor it was an accident,"
says Mr. W.
"I can do jobs to earn money to pay for the window.
Talking with you makes me feel better," says William.
"But I would still like to know
what the worry machine thinks."
"A worry machine is only a machine," says Mr. W.
"It cannot think the way you can.
But you may use it."

15

William whispers his worry to the worry machine.

Mr. W turns the dial.

The worry machine wiggles and whirls.

Mr. W winks one wink.

A white card drops out of the slot.

William reads the card and puts it in his pocket.

He thanks Mr. W and leaves.

"It is amazing how quickly the worry machine can tell you what to do," thinks Mr. W.

Next, Wilma walks into the den.

"I hurt my foot in running practice," says Wilma.

"I can't run in Sunday's race.

I'm worried my team will be angry at me."

"Let's talk and think together," says Mr. W.

"I can't run, but I can cheer for my team," says Wilma.

"That's good thinking," smiles Mr. W.

"May I still use the worry machine?" asks Wilma.

"Yes, but a machine can't think the way you can,"
says Mr. W.

Wilma uses the machine, thanks Mr. W and leaves.

19

Next, Winifred walks into the den.

She tells Mr. W her worry.

They talk and think together.

Winifred likes what she and Mr. W decide to do about her problem.

But she still wants to use the worry machine.

Winifred gets her white card from the worry machine.

She thanks Mr. W and leaves.

"The worry machine always answers so quickly," thinks Mr. W.

"I wonder if the answers help the children?"

21

The following week, William telephones Mr. W.

"My neighbor isn't angry at me," says William.

"What did the worry machine tell you?" asks Mr. W.

"It said, 'Don't Worry'," says William.

"The worry machine helped me a little, but talking
and thinking with you is what really helped me."

"The worry machine told William and me the same thing.
I wonder what it told Wilma?" thinks Mr. W.

That evening, Wilma telephones Mr. W.

"Everything worked out well," says Wilma.

"What did the worry machine tell you?" asks Mr. W.

"It said, 'Don't Worry'," says Wilma.

"The worry machine helped me a little, but talking and thinking with you is what really helped me."

"It is very strange," thinks Mr. W.

"The worry machine told William, Wilma, and me the same thing."

The next day, Winifred finds Mr. W in his kitchen.
"Winifred, what did the worry machine tell you?"
asks Mr. W.
"The worry machine said, 'Don't Worry'," says Winifred.
"The machine told all of us the same thing," says Mr. W.
"And the worry machine was right each time, because
worrying doesn't solve problems."
Suddenly, Winifred and Mr. W hear whirling, whizzing,
wobbling, and whooshing sounds coming from the den.
They rush to see what is happening.

White cards are flying everywhere.

The dial of the worry machine is whirling
round and round.

The worry machine falls apart.

There are bits and pieces everywhere.

Mr. W picks up all the white cards.

He has a strange look on his face.

"Now I know why the worry machine could always answer
so quickly," he says.

"Every card says the same thing: 'Don't Worry.'"

29

"I'll keep all these white cards," says Mr. W.
"They'll remind us not to worry."
"And you'll remind us that talking and thinking
are the best ways to solve problems," smiles Winifred.